Didd

Michael Rothery

Second Revision: November 2020

Weatherdeck Books

Diddle Dee

Copyright © 2020 Michael Rothery
All rights reserved

United Kingdom Licence Notes
The right of Michael Rothery to be identified as the author of this work has been asserted by him in accordance with the Copyrights, Designs and Patents Act 1988

All rights reserved. Apart from any use permitted under UK copyright law no part of this publication may be reproduced, stored in a retrieval system, or transmitted, in any form or by any means, without the prior permission of the publisher.

This is a work of fiction. Names, characters, places, events, and incidents are either the products of the author's imagination or used in a fictitious manner. Any resemblance to actual persons, living or dead, or actual events is purely coincidental and not intended by the author.

ISBN: 9798578398827
Weatherdeck Books

In Memorium

Norma
who kept my notes
from 1983
&
Terry and Doreen
whose beautiful island
inspired the wildlife
elements for
this work of fiction

Contents

Front Matter
Introduction
Beginning
About the Author
Other Books by Mike Rothery

Introduction

In the years following the 1982 Falklands War, a British Naval presence was maintained around the Protectorate with at least two destroyers on task. It was customary to allow small parties of men ashore to spend short periods in 'the camp' or on outlying islands. These visits were always by prior arrangement at the invitation of local people.

The wildlife background to this story is taken from one such visit that I undertook with shipmates to Sea Lion Island in January 1983. At that time the island was a sheep farm owned by Terry and Doreen Clifton. Sadly, both have now passed away. But their two daughters Janet and Marie (who as children acted as our guides during our visit) still live in the Islands.

Sea Lion Island today is a popular wildlife attraction with an airstrip and a lodge for up to 20 visitors.

Diddle-dee jam is still made in the Islands and remains a popular preserve throughout the Falklands and beyond.

M.R.

~.~

1
April 2012

I awoke with a start. Disorientated. The mewing throb in my ears and the gentle rise and fall of my seat bewildered me - it took a moment to recall I was on an aeroplane. It took another to realise what had so jarringly disturbed my sleep. Glancing around, I saw I wasn't the only passenger woken by my daughter's sudden shout of excitement.

'I'm sure it's a whale, Dad,' Heather called again from her seat in front of me. 'Look! Down there,' she urged, jabbing her finger on the plexiglass.

Stifling a yawn, I peered down through my own window and swept the vast expanse of grey, wind-flecked ocean a thousand feet below. I soon picked out what had so excited my daughter, a brown shape occulting among the breaking waves. As I watched, an amorphous white cloud blossomed briefly ahead of the creature before quickly dissipating on the wind. Then, a lesser plume erupted, from a smaller, barely discernible object beside it.

Unclipping, I craned over the seatback where my daughter sat with her nose squashed against the window.

'A pair of sperm whales, mother and calf,' I told her. 'Well spotted.'

'Oh yeah, I can see the calf now.' She pulled back from the window to look up at me with suspicion. 'You're waffling me, Dad. How can you tell they're sperm whales from up here?'

I let out a weary sigh. My daughter, like most sixteen-year-olds, had a healthy disrespect for knowledgeable adults; and when it was me, she had it in spades.

'Well, for starters,' I said, 'she's brown. And look how her head tapers like a finger. And when she blows, she blows out ahead, not straight up. Only sperm whales do that.' I grinned at her, feeling slightly self-conscious – we had aroused the interest of some of our fellow passengers. Heather looked impressed, nodding wisely with a protruding lower lip.

'Believe me now?' I asked her - a slight thickness of emotion in my voice.

She turned to the window, and I slumped back into my seat, ignoring the indulgent smiles from nearby passengers.

'There's a ship down there!' Heather yelled, startling them all once more.

I smiled and closed my eyes.

~.~

As we made our approach across the shoaling water, I pressed my forehead to the window. Streamers of brown kelp raced beneath, while my thoughts flipped between nostalgia and anxiety. The ocean's colour changed suddenly: from iron grey to bright blue to startling aquamarine. Then the transition to landfall: the last glimpse of bright water as a flight of giant petrels scattered away scant feet beneath us; a huddle of large mammals basking on a silver beach, sand dunes, a field of tall tussock mounds, and then, breathtakingly, a green hillside rushing up to meet us.

The aircraft bumped down and bounced once on the grass runway. The twin turbines wound up to a buzz-saw roar, and I pitched forward against the seat belt. Past the window zipped the windsock and the quad of green portacabins that served as the island's air hub, then nothing more manmade, just windswept scrub rolling down to the sea. We gradually slowed sufficiently to turn and backtrack towards the 'terminal'.

Heather's shining face appeared over the back of her seat.

'That was awesome! Did you see those giant seals on the beach?'

I was unable for a moment to speak for grinning. I was touched that my beloved daughter seemed, at last, to be buying-in to this long-delayed project of mine. She had not been keen when I had first broached the subject last Christmas. I shivered as I recalled the tantrum she had thrown – among other things.

When it had seemed safe to re-enter the kitchen, I inspected the back of the door where the heavy saucepan had left a splintered dent. I looked from it to my daughter. Her minute of madness over, she had simply stood there with her chin out defiantly, red-faced and close to tears.

'Was that strictly necessary?' I asked reasonably.

'Oh, Da-ad! What the f— what were you thinking? I'm going with Shelly to their caravan in Cornwall for Easter. I told you weeks ago. *And* you both agreed. Tell him, Mum.'

Helen, always the peacemaker, had laid a calming hand on her shoulder. 'Listen to what your father has to say, sweetheart, just hear him out. Okay? Then, if you really don't want to go …'

My wife glanced at me and gave a helpless shrug.

Heather turned back to me, still mad, still fiercely defiant, but condescending to listen. 'Go on then, convince me that a week on some cold and windy rock in the back of beyond is better than surfing and partying with my best friend in Newquay.'

I had given her my best smile. 'Not *so* cold. It'll be summer down there,' I said. 'Anyway, how about you do both?'

Her eyebrows raised a fraction, challenging me to go on.

'Here's the deal. We'll only be gone the first week, and when we get back, I'll drive you down to Cornwall for your second week with Shelly and Co.'

She had calmed then, though was by no means wholly won over. I spent the next hour telling her about Balsam Island. I showed her my album of photographs from thirty years ago.

(All except one: the one I had hidden away.) Then we looked at the Safari Lodge website. Heather had finally agreed to sleep on it, but I'd seen her interest awaken, and the next morning at breakfast she had given me her grown-up look.

'Okay, Dad.'

It was enough.

'If you think the elephant seals were awesome,' I told her now, 'wait till you see them up close. And you're not supposed to unstrap till we've stopped.'

She ignored me, as usual, and kept her chin and hands defiantly glued to the seatback.

'What is the lodge *really* like?'

I guffawed. 'Thirty years ago, there wasn't even a landing strip here, let alone a lodge. The place was uninhabited then.'

That had been the official line anyway. I shrugged and gave Heather my reassuring Dad look, 'I'm sure it'll be just like their website pictures, all shiny and modern with great food and comfy rooms.'

On the long haul from RAF Brize Norton, I had decided I would tell my daughter the whole disturbing story of this island. It was a story I had not even shared with Helen, my wife of twenty-two years. Our only child was now to carry my secret to the next generation: like a folkloric messenger in a time before writing.

I had almost blurted out the story during our battlefield tour of Goose Green, and again as we stood at the war memorial overlooking San Carlos Water. But now, as the plane drew to a halt on the windblown grass and old memories rose in me like a dark shadow, the telling of it seemed impossible.

We stepped out of the plane's warm cabin into a chill breeze and a heavy overcast: the early-afternoon light sulked under a sky reluctant to admit it was daytime. From somewhere floated the distant cries of seabirds, the faint stink of their guano carried on the breeze. There were ten of us from the aircraft, all bound for the only place in town: an isolated safari lodge on the most isolated island this side of the Antarctic.

A minibus took us up to the lodge, bumping up a winding trail paved with uneven stones. A deep-green tangle of weeds carpeted the treeless slopes on either side, adding to the gloomy mood of the place. Our baggage had been loaded onto a trailer which a grumbling quadbike was now towing behind us.

Nobody spoke. All the convivial chatter of the short flight from Stanley had dried up. Heather too seemed to have fallen under the spell of the island's melancholy; her lively enthusiasms had ended the moment she had stepped off the aircraft. She returned my encouraging smile with a glare that said: *'What have you brought me to?'*

I leaned in and whispered, 'It'll be good, I promise.'

'Yeah, right,' she muttered, looking away.

Our first sight of the lodge was a grey pantiled roof as we rounded a corner of the hill. Then, topping a short rise, a giant dish-aerial came into view. Our bus pulled up under the covered entrance of a single-storey modern building: marble-faced walls with a portico of polished pine. The enormous satellite dish dominated a well-tended lawn opposite. Panoramic windows and discreet lighting imbued the lobby with a bright, airy feel that contrasted with the gloom outside. The simple lounge furniture arranged on a quarry tiled floor spoke of functional elegance. Heather and I found ourselves first in line at the reception desk.

'Good afternoon, and welcome to Balsam Island.'

The woman was an attractive forty-something. Her name-badge told me she was 'Lynda'.

'Hi,' I said, returning Lynda's corporate smile with pressed lips and sliding my online booking printout across the desk. 'We are—'

'Oh, cool!' chimed in Heather behind me, 'they've got WIFI.' I glanced around to see her engrossed in her phone, already thumbing away to her friends. Noticing my rolled eyes, the receptionist flashed a grimace of allegiance; *teenagers, huh?*

Lynda was as well-groomed as any big-city hotel receptionist, which seemed vaguely incongruous on this remote island. But then I remembered how much it was costing.

'Ah, yes, Mr Brown. And er … you must be Heather?' Heather granted Lynda a quick grin then returned to her screen where a new message had just pinged in. At the same time, my own phone buzzed in my pocket: an incoming text, probably from Helen. I ignored it for now – I would call her from our room.

'You are in the family suite, Mr Brown. Our most popular – you'll just *adore* the view.' She placed two plastic key-cards on the booking sheet and slid it back to me. 'You're at the very end of the corridor to your left, south-facing.'

I thought for a moment, then said: 'That view you mentioned: East Jowett Bay?'

Lynda's face came suddenly alight. '*That's right!* You know the island?'

I stumbled for an answer. 'Er, a few years ago. You know, before all this? …' I twirled a finger vaguely.

That seemed to have stumped her. Aware that the people behind me were getting impatient, I picked up my keycards. Heather looked up from her phone. 'Let's go dump our stuff, Dad, and go check out those elephant seals.' Her reconnection with social media had brought about a miraculous recovery of spirits.

'Just hold your horses, sweetheart, let's get settled in first, then we'll see.'

But Lynda had not yet finished with us: 'I just need to remind you, Sir: guests are advised to remain in the Lodge until they have attended the "Welcome and Safety Briefing".'

I gave her the eyebrow. 'Which is at … ?'

'Four-o-clock, Sir, in the Sealion Lounge.'

'Okay, fine. We'll be there.'

'Aww, Dad?' whined Heather.

Lynda turned to Heather – her smile vanished, 'Seals might seem slow and clumsy on shore, but you need to remember they're wild animals. They can be unpredictable. Even a two-ton elephant seal can move quickly when it wants to. That's one reason we ask all our visitors to attend the short safety presentation by our wardens before venturing out alone.'

Heather sighed resignedly. 'Okay, whatever.'

Lynda motioned her forward and leaned in. 'I know just how you feel, I was the same when I first came here. Trust me, you'll enjoy it more when you've rested up after your long journey, and you won't be disappointed. You're in for a treat, I promise you.'

To my relief, Heather responded with her grown-up face and smiled bravely. Just then, her phone rang.

'Hi, Mum … yeah, we just arrived—'

With the phone glued to her ear, she retired to a settee by the windows.

'In the meantime,' Lynda continued, 'the bar and restaurant are open for you to have a drink or order afternoon tea. I hope you both enjoy your stay with us.'

By the time I had showered and spoken to Helen, and Heather had claimed her bedroom - arranging her things 'to make it hers' – it was almost two-thirty.

I picked up my parka and said, 'If I'm not back by four make sure you go to the briefing, and please, listen to what they say, don't sit there texting or plugged into Two Directions.'

'It's *One* Direction, philistine! Where you off to, anyway?'

'For a little walk. I'll be back in an hour or so.'

'But that woman said…'

'Look, I'm not going far, and I won't be going anywhere near the shore.' I took a deep breath, 'I'm just going to take a walk to where the old sheep farm used to be, it's a personal thing, a bit of nostalgia. I'd like to do it alone.'

She looked crestfallen and seemed suddenly very young. Was I right to have brought her here, to this place of such complex personal memories? I walked over and gave her a hug.

'It's just this one time, Sweetie,' I assured her gently. 'After that, I'm all yours. Okay?'

She pouted for a moment, then brightened.

'Okay, Dad, cool. Can I have a drink from the bar?'

'No alcohol,' I warned sternly.

'Spoilsport,' she scowled and flopped onto her bed, causing me a chuckle. I doubted they'd serve her booze anyway; she was small for sixteen and looked younger. I left her tapping happily on her phone, nodding away to whatever racket her earbuds were delivering.

~·~

I was gratified to find a dramatic improvement in the weather. Gone was the dark blanket that had earlier so dampened my daughter's heart. The few remaining clouds were feathery fragments scudding high against a blaze of kingfisher blue.

With a fresh westerly breeze and the warm sunshine on my back, I set off down a narrow dirt track between ankle-deep shrubs bearing bright and plentiful red berries. I swept up a handful. They tasted sweeter, less tart than I remembered. But then it had been December: Spring, in the southern hemisphere. Now, in April, the fruits were older, and past their best.

At a small lake -- which I now recalled was known as Otter Pond -- I stopped to watch a small flock of teal gliding gently on its rippling waters. I caught a vaguely remembered scent on the breeze: sweet vanilla. And there, beyond the freshwater tarn by the edge of the low cliffs, I spotted the source: the aromatic stands of balsam bog. The white-flowered plinths were like many iterations of Granny's parlour table, their lace-like coverings resplendent in the golden light of the lowering sun.

These icons of their eponymous Island made me think of Nobbay, and I grinned. I wondered what he and Frank had done with their lives. I imagined Nobbay slogging away in some engineering factory in Birmingham and looking forward to retirement. I had heard that Frank had signed up for a professional rugby club in South Wales, but he had not appeared in the public sporting eye and was more-than-likely too old now even to play. I wondered if my two shipmates had broken our covenant. I doubted it somehow. Who would believe them?

I walked up to the next ridge, looked down to the eastern end of the island and pictured the scene as it had been then. The coarse grasses and wiry shrubs had grown back to conceal any trace of the homestead that had once occupied this lonely plot. Gone now were the farm buildings and the shabby little house with its red tin roof. Gone too was the bunkhouse where once, in a time out of memory, itinerant shearers were housed. Gone was the barn where peat logs were dried, and where an ancient tractor had been sheltered. All had been bulldozed away by the company who now owned the island. Only the tattered and faded windsock remained, flying near horizontal in the stiffening breeze, like a fingerpost, pointing to the past.

A great skua passed low over my head, heading toward the sea to feed, tolerant of my presence because her fledgelings had long flown. In the Spring, it had been different. Then it was a place bursting with new life, a cacophony of protective sound and energy, a primaeval charge in the air that only now in its absence recollected itself to me. But it was also a place of death; the bones and dried-out carcasses of nature's discards. And something else … beyond the naturalists' explanations.

I continued down the slope toward the site where it all started, and rising like a spectre, the memories returned.

~.~

2
December 1982

Buster resisted the urge to close his eyes as the helicopter skimmed over the long ocean rollers, clipping along at gut-wrenching speed.

'Nasty looking squall over there at ten o clock. Looks like it's converging on the island.'

The scratchy voice in Buster's helmet belonged to the man in front, in the seat next to the pilot. Lieutenant Commander Steve Ogilvy had been glancing anxiously between his radar scanner and the worsening weather ahead.

The island was a flat lozenge far on the western horizon. Isolated pillows of cumulous scudded low and darkling in the afternoon sky: squalls hung with slanting curtains of sleet. It was one of these, a particularly dark and threatening cloud, that was giving the Observer concern.

'Seven miles to run,' the pilot replied. 'We should get there before it. It'll need to be a quick turnaround, though. Alright, guys?'

Buster looked across at his two companions in the back. Both nodded.

'Yes, Sir. Were all set,' he assured the pilot.

A hotchpotch of startled seabirds on the water ahead flapped frantically to get airborne. The Lynx slowed over a patch turquoise water, then crossed a silver beach where a herd of elephant seals craned their massive necks to the unaccustomed noise.

'Get everyone ready in the back, PO,' Ogilvy said, 'make sure you've all got your kit to hand. As soon as the wheels touch, unstrap, secure your helmets to the seats then pile out with your stuff. Don't leave anything behind, we won't be hanging about.'

'Ok Boss, no problem,' Buster said. Nobbay and Frank both stuck up thumbs in acknowledgement: Buster was the only one with a helmet mic.

'And have a good break,' Ogilvy added, straining around in his seat to look at the three men. 'Wish I was coming with you.'

Buster and Frank managed sympathetic grins, but Nobbay could not entirely hide his horror: nobody wanted an officer along.

A small group of buildings came into sight, one with a bright red roof, the others rust-brown. Near them, an orange windsock lifted in the strengthening breeze. The pilot turned the aircraft to windward and brought it to an ungainly hover before dropping to land, then applied negative lift. As the helicopter hunkered down, Buster slid back his door and slung out the heavy Bergens as Frank handed them to him. Jumping out onto the scrubby grass, he grabbed one of the backpacks and ran clear of the rotor disc, buffeted by the downdraught and wincing at the turbine noise. Once clear, he turned to watch Frank and Nobbay disembark and scoop up the other two packs. The helicopter lifted off the moment they were all clear - a farewell wave from the Observer - and headed back towards the ship -- invisible now over the murky horizon.

The wind tugged fiercely at the men as they stripped off their life-jackets and immersion suits. Already the first splashes of driven sleet struck sharp and cold as they struggled into foul-weather gear. When Frank donned a fur hat, Buster looked up at it and grinned.

'What d'you reckon, Nobbay? Does Frank look the part … er, sorry, I meant *a* part.'

The diminutive Brummy adjusted his uniform beret and gave a nervous laugh, preoccupied with the zip of his arctic jacket.

'Bollocks to you both!' growled the big Welshman.

Buster's humour died suddenly. He felt goosebumps as he realised they were not alone. He nudged the Welshman. 'Looks like we've got company,' he murmured, nodding to where a man and a woman stood in the doorway of the house.

Suddenly, a heavily clad young child ducked past the adults and bounded out towards the men. Her excited giggling was all that told she was a girl. Her beaming face was ruddy, her cheeks cracked and weathered, her brown hair butchered in a ragged attempt at a bob. Behind her, a slightly larger figure followed at a more measured pace. The girls were identically dressed in crudely-stitched woollen dungarees over chunky, grey-checked shirts and clumsy-looking work boots. Their countenances were so alike they had to have been sisters. As the sleet intensified, both girls pulled up woolly hoods. With the coverings laced tightly around their red faces, the pair resembled consecutively-sized Russian dolls.

Up at the house, the man and woman watched passively from the doorway: both were smiling. The woman was attractive, despite the dowdy clothing and woolly headscarf. The man, slightly shorter than his wife, had a pinched face under a wide-brimmed cap with a slick of black hair hanging over his brow. Oddly, neither gave any show of concern that their children were approaching three strangers. The woman gave them a little wave, and Buster raised a hand in acknowledgement.

That was when the world froze.

Buster grabbed the frame of his Bergen for support as a wave of inexplicable wretchedness washed over him. His head swam. The whitened scene suddenly split, like two images becoming unfocussed: one retaining the present reality, the other, drained of all colour, a dreary imitation in sepia. In that stilled moment, a desperate longing seemed to emanate from all around: not the vague yearning for home that occasionally invaded private moments onboard. This was the visceral certainty of some awful, impending tragedy.

Then Buster became aware of the delighted child rushing to greet them, and the weird sensation left him as quickly as it had come. Straightening, he wondered if he had imagined it—a touch of land-sickness, perhaps. Stepping onto firm ground after months at sea in heavy weather could be disorientating. Frank looked a little shaken, but that could have been the shock of this unexpected encounter.

Nobbay was fiddling with the zip of his foul-weather jacket which had become stuck. The sleet was by now sweeping in almost horizontal on the bitingly cold wind and remodelling the marine engineer in white. He swore loudly as his frozen fingers slipped off the fastener

'Hey, ladies present!' growled Frank.

Nobbay looked up and reddened. 'Sorry,' he said, then resorted to red-faced grunting as he jerked and tugged once more at the stubborn zip.

The Welshman grinned down at the child. 'You'll have to excuse our friend, he's a bit …' he twirled a finger by his ear, 'you know?'

Nobbay walked off a pace and renewed his efforts to free the jammed zip.

'Have you come to find us?' the little girl asked, then spun around and laughed delightedly into the wind.

That unexpected laughter was such a blithe, enchanting sound that even the pre-occupied Nobbay looked up in surprise.

Buster noticed Frank grow suddenly maudlin, a faraway look on his face. He knew the Welshman had two young children of his own, whom he doted on and wouldn't be seeing for another four months.

'Looks like we have,' replied the big man, beaming down at the child. 'So, is it my turn to hide, now?'

The girl spun around once more in her clumsy pirouette and laughed again. She seemed oblivious to the lashing sleet which stung the faces of the three men.

'Not yet you haven't' she said, teasingly.

The girl was maybe eleven years old, and Buster now saw she would be cherubically pretty if it were not for her weather-scarred face.

'We weren't expecting you,' she said earnestly, glancing down at the men's baggage. 'Where did you come from, and how did you get here?'

'Er, we're the Navy?' Nobbay supplied, pointing to his beret badge before attending once more to his jacket zipper.

The little girl's expression creased with incomprehension. Buster and Frank exchanged puzzled glances. Frank dropped to one knee in front of the girl, causing Buster a worried glance up to the house. But the two adults were no longer there.

Bloody hell! What kind of parents would leave their children alone with three strange men?

'What's your name, sweetheart?' the Welshman asked gently.

The girl smiled shyly and said in almost a whisper, 'It's Jennifer, really. But you can call me Jenny.'

'Well, Jenny, my name's Frank. Now, did you see a helicopter landing here a few minutes ago?'

She looked back blankly, then shook her head.

'Okay, but you heard a big noise just now, yes?'

'No, she didn't,' snapped the bigger girl arriving at the scene. 'Because there wasn't one.' With an accusing glance at Frank, she took her sister by the hand, 'C'mon, Jenny, we have to go.'

'Now, just a minute,' Buster said. 'That makes no sense. I mean, you must have at least heard the helicopter just now.'

The girl ignored him and continued dragging her sister toward the house.

'But they've come to find us,' insisted Jenny, trying to pull back against her sister's firm grasp.

Buster ran to catch them up. 'Look, Miss. We're Royal Navy, and our ship's out there somewhere,' he explained, pointing roughly eastwards. 'And I have to go and introduce us to your Dad and apologise for not radioing ahead.'

'Oh, he won't mind,' the elder girl murmured, then turned quickly to face him.

'So… why *are* you here?' She demanded. Then, her eyes widened. 'Have you *really* come to find us?'

'Yes—they—have,' squealed Jenny. 'Pleeease, Pammy, let's just *talk* to them.'

All this talk of coming to find them seemed nonsensical to Buster. Had they interrupted some childish game?

Frank walked up to lend support, leaving the hapless Nobbay still swearing as he struggled to free his jacket zipper.

'Look, girls, we're not here to make trouble for you or your family. We've just come for a bit of a leg-stretch and a look at your fantastic wildlife.' The Welshman's battered features had softened in a way Buster hadn't seen before. The Navy's champion prop-forward had taken on the homely demeanour of somebody's dad.

And it seemed to have done the trick, for Pammy paused, stared at the two men thoughtfully, then said, somewhat assertively, 'You can stay in the bunkhouse, bring your bags, I'll show you.' With that, she turned and began to stroll briskly down the hill, still dragging her little sister.

'Whoa, hold up there,' Buster called, catching up with the pair again.

Suddenly, the wind dropped. The icy downpour ceased as if someone had turned off a tap. Buster looked up at the miracle of a blue sky and threw back his hood. He turned to the older sister.

'Thanks, young lady. Your offer's appreciated. But we're self-contained. We brought camping gear.'

'You'll be better off in the bunkhouse,' the younger girl sang out, looking up at the hillside where fresh squall clouds were gathering. 'Dad lets visitors use it -- when we're not shearing that is.'

Pammy had stopped but was clearly still bent on heading for the bunkhouse - as if it were a done deal. Buster looked at Frank, who just shrugged and said, 'You're Team Leader, mate, your call.'

Nobbay - with his jacket still unzipped and his woolly-pulley glistening with frozen sleet - had a pleading look on his face.

Buster relented with a sigh, 'Wait for us, Pammy, we'll get our Bergens.'

Presently, all five were marching down the hill in a line towards a low, isolated structure. Nobbay, bringing up the rear, had given up on his zip. He had been puzzling at something the younger child had said, and now called ahead in his uncompromising West Midlands twang.

'Hey, Jennay, what happens in the bunkhouse when you're shearing?'

The little girl gave no reply, just threw the diminutive marine engineer a backwards glance as if not sure if he had been joking.

~.~

3

The three men followed the sisters past a dilapidated barn and over a short tract of trampled grass. The little one now broke free of her sister and skipped back to the men and took up station alongside Frank.

'Were you all in the war?' she asked brightly, looking up with the earnestness of innocence.

Nobody replied. They just exchanged mutually-understood glances. The war had ended seven months ago with the Argentinian's surrender in Port Stanley. Each of the three Petty Officers was silenced by his individual memories of those terrible days in San Carlos.

For Buster, it was the dimmed intensity of the Ops Room, perhaps the only place you get the 'big picture', and where you see first-hand the unravelling of order. *And* the fates of the unlucky. Frank, one of the ship's two Radio Supervisors, saw *his* war through naked eyes and in the frantic fog of communications traffic. But Buster knew - and suspected even Frank would acknowledge - that Nobbay's experience was the more chilling. For the men watching events, the action had ebbed and flowed. But the terror among those locked-down below the waterline had been relentless.

Pammy dropped back and told her sister, 'You know you're not supposed to ask about the war. People don't like it.'

Jenny wrinkled her nose. 'But I only—'

'Shut up!' snapped Pammy.

Buster suppressed a grin.

The bunkhouse proved to be a long wooden hut; a narrow stoop at the nearest gable end with two steps up.

Pammy went ahead and entered the building. The little one, unable to help herself, tugged on Frank's sleeve and whispered urgently, 'Dad was at Vimy Ridge. *He* never talks about it, either.'

'It's not something any of us talk about much, sweetheart. But the Argies didn't come all the way out here, surely?'

The girl gave him an odd look and ran into the hut to join her sister.

'Where the hell's Vimy Ridge?' Frank said, turning to the other two, 'I never heard of it.'

'Me neither,' Buster agreed. His brow furrowed. The name seemed to ring a bell, but he couldn't place it. 'Ah. I reckon she must've meant *Wireless* Ridge.'

'Well their old man couldn't have been there, anyway,' Nobbay said. 'How could that have worked?'

'No, you're right,' agreed Frank. 'So, maybe he was just telling stories to his kids. Let's have a shufti at where we're sleeping tonight.'

Nobbay was first up onto the narrow porch, holding the door handle and repeatedly throwing his shoulder at the door to little effect. Frank stepped up behind him

'Move aside, Mere Mortal,' he growled. The door creaked and distorted under the big man's weight, but still refused to yield.

'*Bloody hell!* It's stuck.'

'Who knew?' Nobbay muttered, which won him a withering glare.

'What's up, Big Man,' goaded Buster, grinning hugely. 'Missed your wheaties this morning?'

The Welshman cast him a desperate look then drew back and shouldered the door more determinedly. The whole structure shook, and the door burst open under a protest of rusted hinges.

'Phew!' grunted Frank, 'that shifted it.'

'The kids opened it easily enough,' observed Nobbay.

'Talking of whom, where the hell have they gone?' wondered Frank, entering first.

Clouds of musty-smelling dust rose under their boots as the three tramped inside. Suspended motes glinted in sunlight beaming in from small grimy windows set high in the sidewalls. Six iron-framed beds occupied the right-hand side, each topped with a grubby mattress. The remainder of the space formed a communal area: a large, solid-looking wooden table stood at its centre with six chairs lined against the left-hand wall.

'Look, there's a door at the other end,' said Nobbay. 'They must have gone back home.'

'That's weird,' said Buster, walking the length of the hut, stepping gingerly to avoid raising more dust. As he went, he took stock of the amenities. Beyond the table, a stone plinth supported a small, potbellied stove. Beside it was a box filled with shards of wood for kindling. There was also a heap of what had once been peat logs, now crumbled away and useless.

At the far end was a small utility-room containing cleaning equipment and a toilet; the bowl was half-filled with dried peat dust – at least Buster hoped it was peat. To the left of this was the kitchen space: a Belfast Sink, a stone worktop, and a small food cupboard. The door Nobbay had spotted was in a recess to the right, and bore a faded notice marked 'Fire Escape'. It opened grudgingly to the outside, with three concrete steps down to the grass.

'Yeah, I guess you're right, Nobbay,' he called, but with little conviction. Something was not right. He left the door open to let in the freshening breeze.

'No light switches,' observed Nobbay.

'I suppose that's 'cos there is no lights,' Frank retorted, somewhat sardonically.

'No probs,' said Buster, pointing out the line of hooks hanging from the ceiling. 'We'll hang the Tilley lamps from those.'

Although in need of a thorough clean up, their unplanned quartering was not far from perfect, and the men quickly applied themselves to making it habitable.

While Frank shook the wool-stuffed mattresses out on the porch and began dusting and sweeping, Buster busied himself at the kitchen area. The water from the tap ran dirty brown at first but cleared after a minute or two. Then he tasted it cautiously. It had a slightly brackish flavour but would probably be okay after boiling.

Nobbay, whose expertise was in all things plumbing and mechanical, took charge of the dysfunctional toilet. After half an hour of grunting and swearing, he let out a great whoop of joy as the toilet flushed.

In a box under the worktop, Buster found an assortment of cooking containers.

'Great, there's a kettle,' he announced. 'I'll wet the tea.'

From his bergen, he pulled out the portable gas stove and a box of teabags. Presently, the three shipmates sat around the table, cupping their cold hands around mugs of tea and munching jammy dodgers. They spoke in raised voices over a wind that now howled angrily once more, this time bringing volleys of hailstones rattling on the tin roof of the bunkhouse.

'Looks like we dropped lucky,' Frank offered.

'Yeah, it wouldn't a been much fun under canvas in this,' Nobbay said, jerking up a thumb to the clatter overhead.

'Probably why those girls were in such a hurry to get home,' enjoined the Welshman.

'Probably,' agreed Buster, distractedly.

Nobbay said, 'All the same, call this R an' R? Don't see why we couldn't just have called in somewhere for a proper run ashore?'

Frank stared at him, then cleared his throat ominously. 'And where the bleeding hell do you suppose that would be, shit-for-brains, Buenos Aires? I'm sure they'd welcome us *there* with open arms. Port Stanley's still a flipping shambles, and there's nowhere else in these godforsaken islands suitable for a ship alongside.'

'Hey!' said Buster. 'Let's just cool it, eh?'

Frank looked at their designated team leader and visibly calmed. With a great sigh, he leaned his big frame across the table and told Nobbay: 'Just drink yer tea, mate, and stop talking like a Brummie twerp.'

Nobbay looked subdued and nervous. Since San Carlos, the PO Stoker had developed a tic under his right eye that now twitched uncontrollably. He sipped his tea, then took a deep breath which got the attention of his companions. His cheek had ceased twitching as he looked the Welshman firmly in the eye.

'Oi ain't a Brummay. Oim frum the Black Countray.'

Frank stared back at him in shock for a moment, then his vast shoulders began to shake with mirth. Buster too looked ready to burst into fits. Nobbay looked from one to the other, his weasel face creased with genuine puzzlement.

'What's so funnay?' he asked.

At this, both men fell into helpless laughter.

Frank stood up, shaking his head, his face still flushed with humour. He picked up Nobbay's arctic jacket from where he had thrown it in frustration. He fiddled a moment with the fastener, succeeded in pulling up the zip, then handed it to its owner.

'Trick is with these arctics, Bach, to pull the slider fully home first.'

'Thank yo,' said Nobbay grudgingly, taking his jacket and trying the zip for himself.

Smiling ruefully, Frank clapped a big hand on his shoulder. 'Sorry, mate. Didn't mean to have a go at you. I guess you're alright, for a grease-monkey.'

~.~

4

After tea, the three shipmates donned foulies and strolled downhill under a cloudless sky towards the beach they had flown over on the way in. Myriad seabirds soared overhead, their strident calls merging with the distant crashing of waves; a faint smell of guano and seaweed carried on the chill breeze. The ankle-high grass was still damp from the squall: the men's hiking boots crunched over heaps of hailstones that lay glistening among its coarse blades.

The unexpected comfort of a roof under which to spend this one precious night ashore had brought a mood of buoyancy to the shipmates. The sun warmed their backs and spirits were high; Frank and Nobbay chatted amiably as they walked.

But despite the companionable mood, Buster had a nagging concern. At their briefing onboard they were told the island had been abandoned years ago. Therefore, the presence here of a farming family had come as an embarrassing shock.

Mulling over the possible consequences of coming here uninvited, he was assailed once more by the same wave of wretchedness he had experienced after landing. He missed his step and reeled as the sunlit scene bifurcated and a sepia reproduction hovered mysteriously alongside. For a moment, the world seemed in stasis, and a feeling of imminent tragedy seemed to tug at his very soul.

'What's up, Bach?'

Frank's concerned query sounded distant, though the big man was walking close-by, and Buster was aware of a supporting hand at his elbow. His senses suddenly cleared, and reality imposed itself once more.

Nobbay was also watching him and frowning. 'Yo've gone all pale, Buster,' he said, 'Yo takin' a turn?'

'I'm okay, it's just—' Buster paused and studied their two faces. 'This is going to sound weird, but did either of you feel something just now? Like … like the world shifted – like something bad was going to happen?'

Frank looked thoughtful for a moment, then said, 'Now you come to mention it, Bach, I did get an odd feeling of unrealness for a second. I just put it down to being on land for the first time in months. It gets you like that sometimes, doesn't it?'

Nobbay shook his head. 'Well, nothing like that happened to—Hey, look. Those kids are coming over.'

The trio halted and watched the children's' approach. The two girls were converging from their left, the bigger one, Pammy striding purposefully. Her sister skipped gaily by her side.

'Hiya, Girls,' beamed the Welshman. 'You come to join our expedition?'

'We've come to *guide* you, *of course*,' squealed Jenny. 'In case Scary Sam's on the beach, cos he'll *bite you and tear you all to bits*.'

The three men grinned at the little girl's play of ferociousness.

'Ooh, Scary Sam sounds terrifying,' said Frank. 'Well, you'd better come and look after us then. Right lads?'

'Oh, yes!' grinned Buster. 'Getting torn to bits could really spoil our day.'

'What's Scary Sam?' asked Nobbay.

'He's a big male sea lion,' Pammy supplied. 'But take no notice of her. Sam won't be down there now. He's with his females on the other end of the island.'

'But there's the elephants,' Jenny countered brightly. 'And they're *hu--uge*!' She spread her small arms to emphasise the animals' hugeness.

'Elephants?' said Nobbay incredulously.

'She means elephant seals,' Pammy explained.

'Oh, okay,' said Nobbay. 'We saw them from the helicopter.'

The little one tugged at her sister's sleeve, '*That's* what that big man said before, Pammy: a heli—er … thingummy.'

Pammy turned to Nobbay and asked, 'What's a helicopter?'

Nobbay spluttered. 'Don't yo know wh—'

'It's a kind of aeroplane,' interrupted Buster, throwing a warning glance at the engineer.

'Er, guys, let's get going if we're going,' urged Frank, looking at his watch. 'Sunset in three hours.'

The walk recommenced.

'I'm Pam by the way, and this small annoying person is my sister, Jenny.'

Frank did the honours with introductions.

'This fella's called Buster. He's from Cambridge, that's why he talks posh.'

Buster guffawed, 'He's just saying that because he's Welsh and isn't used to proper English. And just so's you know, I don't come from Cambridge, I live in the Cambridgeshire Fens.'

'A swampy then,' the Welshman jibed, 'just as bad, I'd say. And this little squirt is Nobbay, he's from Birmingham.'

'Tipton, actually,' corrected Nobbay. 'And that's not classed as Birmingham.'

'And me? I'm Frank, a reject from the Rhondda Valley, that's in Wales if you didn't know.'

'Why've you got funny names?' Jenny piped up.

The three exchanged bemused glances before Nobbay took up the explanation. 'It's traditional, see? Nobbay's not my real name, it's Peter actually. My nickname's supposed to be Nobby: Nobby Hall, see. But they all likc taking the mick outa me accent, so they call me Nobbay, y'see. Buster here is Buster 'cuz his name's Brown – Buster Brown. His real name is … er, actually, I don't know his real name.'

27

'Vincent,' Buster supplied, 'Vince for short.'

'And what about Frank?' Jenny asked, turning to the big Welshman.

'Oh, that's what me mum called me,' said Frank, 'cos I'm honest and always tell the truth.' He gave them an avuncular wink, drawing a delighted giggle from the little one and an eye-roll from her sister.

The ground flora grew gradually denser: coarse heathers and red-berried shrubs sometimes reaching knee-height. Pam scanned the sky ahead.

'We have to be a bit careful here,' she advised.

'Especially Frank,' Jenny added gleefully, looking up at the Welshman's fur hat.

Buster suppressed a smile. He recognised the behaviour of the birds ahead, crying shrilly and swooping low over the swaying shrubbery

The first sortie came suddenly.

'What the …' exclaimed Frank, as the fur hat was torn from his head.

The marauding bird carried it a little way before dropping it. Little Jenny squealed and pirouetted delightedly as the big Welshman ran to retrieve his much-loved hat. Before long, several more birds appeared and began diving at the men.

'Sod off, you f… flippin' shite hawk,' squealed Nobbay, ducking an attempt at his beret.

'They're skuas, actually,' corrected Pam, walking calmly alongside, her shorter stature apparently protecting her from the aerial attacks. 'They get quite aggressive at this time of year.'

'They're only defending their chicks,' added Jenny. 'They nest on the ground, you know, *stupid* things.' She performed another of her pirouettes.

'Don't see too many trees around here,' observed Nobbay drily. 'Looks like they ain't got too much ch-- Whoa!' He flinched as a webbed talon swept dangerously past his ear.

'How come you two ain't getting it?' he asked, stuffing his beret into his pocket.

'Because they go for the tallest,' said Pam, grinning cheekily. 'That's why we're walking next to you big people.'

'Tip of the day,' Nobbay chirped up gleefully. 'Stay by me Frank, I'll look after you.'

Nobbay was a foot shorter than the Welshman.

'Where'd you learn that trick,' Frank asked Buster.

The fenland man had his own technique for dealing with the aggressive seabirds. He walked along with one hand in the air, then pulled it down at the last moment so that the attacker passed well clear overhead.

'From my Dad, when I was a kid' Buster replied. 'We used to go to the Farne Islands to watch the terns.'

'Oh, yeah,' he said. 'Forgot you was a bit of a twitcher... Ooh, you bugger!'

Once again Frank's fur hat was swept off his head. When he re-joined the group after retrieving it, Buster chuckled, 'Even the birds think you look a right plonker in that hat.'

The Welshman laughed good-naturedly. 'Seen a lot of sea time, this ole bonnet o mine.'

'Try this yourself, Big Man,' Buster advised, his hand raised as another skua lined up to attack. 'Then you might get to keep your "ole bonnet" a bit longer.'

The aerial harassment tailed off as they passed out of the nesting site onto an uneven tract of firm, sandy ground all but denuded of vegetation.

'What the *hell* is that noise?' Frank said as a mad cacophony of braying began up ahead.

'Jackasses,' Jenny announced proudly.

'We'll have to hold our noses in a bit,' Pam warned. 'The jackasses smell *really* bad.'

'Yo ain't got donkeys!' Nobbay exclaimed disbelievingly.

Buster snorted a laugh.

He was starting to feel a kind of living pulse about the island, an electric zing that infected everything around. It was, he knew, the effects of the fruitful season and the bringing forth of new life. But the Fenlander had never felt it so powerfully.

'No, of course not,' Jenny replied, frowning at Nobbay.

'Why would we want donkeys?' Pam asked him.

'We had *horses* once!' Jenny interjected. 'Before we got the tractor…'

Frank clapped Nobbay on the shoulder. 'Oh, mate,' he laughed. 'You should have paid attention in the briefing. They were talking about jackass *penguins*.'

'…then we ate 'em,' added Jenny morosely.

'*Big* mouth,' scolded her sister.

The little party moved on with the engineer shaking his head in bewilderment.

'Elephants and jackasses,' he muttered. 'What's a bloke to think?'

As the racket increased, so did the sharp odour of guano. Up to now, nobody had seen the birds responsible for the noise. But then Buster, leading the single file, pulled up suddenly. The diminutive figure brayed loudly at him while bravely standing her ground a mere two feet away.

'Keep your distance,' Pam murmured from behind, 'She's got chicks - look over to your left.'

Buster looked, and there, sure enough, in a burrow entrance, a pair of youngsters huddled. Fluffy balls of cuteness in brown and white, they sat looking on - seemingly unperturbed – as their parent valiantly defended her domain. Noticing a sudden rise in the ambient mayhem, Buster looked up to find the entire population had come out to join the protest.

The penguin colony sloped down to a bank of grass-topped dunes some fifty yards ahead. Its lateral extents were vast and impossible to measure by eye.

'The elephants are this way,' Jenny shouted above the din, leaping past the mother who lunged vainly at the girl's flying feet.

As the stench grew eye-wateringly intense; the self-appointed guides hurried their visitors through the colony, dodging and weaving their way through the hordes of squalling penguins. The party descended to the windswept dune, then careened down the soft sand onto the seashore. Here, beyond the deadening dune, only the lazy cries of circling seabirds and the rhythmic tumble of waves dominated the soundscape.

But, despite the lessened noise level, they found the beach as densely populated as the pandemonium they had just vacated. The difference here: the animals were enormous. Some were at least fifteen feet long, their flaccid bodies flattened under their own immense weight. Many were in the advanced stages of catastrophic moulting. Swathes of fur hung from their long bodies, leaving exposed areas vulnerable.

Indeed, one animal rippled and groaned as a raptor hacked away at its back like some demonic jockey. At the group's approach, the vexed mammal heaved its ungainly mass up on two flippered limbs, causing the avian rider to squawk and flap on its grisly mount. The elephant seal turned a pair of watery eyes on the intruders. Opening a cavernous pink maw under its uncurled trunk, it gave a muted roar. Having thus lodged its protest, the monstrous animal settled back down as if exhausted by the effort. It stared dolefully at the men and snorted into the sand, resigning itself to both the human intrusion and the carnage being wreaked upon its back. A trickle of bright new blood oozed from the wound.

Buster took out his camera and snapped off a couple of pictures.

'What bird is that, Pam?' asked Nobbay.

'It's a caracara, but we call 'em—'

Just then, Jenny ran past her, waving her arms at the predator and approaching perilously close to the tormented giant.

'Bugger *off*, Johnny Rook!' she cried.

The caracara flapped onto a nearby rock from where it glared at the little girl accusingly.

'Johnny Rooks,' Pam finished with a sigh. 'Come away, Jenny.'

'I hate it when they do that,' Jenny said heatedly, returning to her sister's side. 'I like elephants, they're my friends.'

'Yeah, I can see that' Buster said. 'But your sister's right. You shouldn't get so close.'

Then, to his astonishment, the little girl ran up to another of the adult bulls. Without hesitation, she vaulted onto its back to straddle the beast, then sat there looking pleased with herself. The bull seemed unmoved, he merely grunted and snorted a little, then settled down as if it was perfectly normal to have a human on his back.

'I keep telling her not to do that,' said Pam, 'it can be dangerous. One of our shearers once got crushed underneath one.'

'That one seems fairly calm,' observed Buster.

'Yeah, they seem to tolerate the little minx for some reason.'

'Go on, Nobbay, give it a go,' Frank said, 'you know you want to.'

Nobbay, who'd been looking on open-mouthed at the little girl's reckless behaviour, harrumphed and said, 'Yeah, right.'

'The rooks have a go at our sheep too,' Pam told the men. 'Especially at lambing.'

'Yeah, I was wondering about that,' Buster said. 'Where *are* your sheep?'

'We moved 'em to the fresh tussac over in East Jowett,' Pam explained. 'It's all grazed up this end and needs a season to grow back.'

The Welshman asked, 'How many sheep you got, Pam?'

'Ooh, about three thousand.'

Buster wondered again how the briefing could have got it so wrong. They really should not have come to a working sheep farm without permission from the owner. Parking the problem, for now, he switched his attention to other points of interest: the abundant variety of birds.

A short walk along the beach, beyond the seal colony, lay an ornithologist's dream. Birds dotted the silver sand in their hundreds; small flocks of two-banded plovers darted back and forth at the water's edge. Oyster-catchers circled low between sea and sand, their fluted calls attenuated on the breeze. Many more species swooped and glided in the clear sapphire sky of early summer. This was not an opportunity to be missed.

He walked to a cluster of rocks and sat down. From his rucksack, he fished out his camera, binoculars, pocket field guide and notebook, then got to work recording what he saw.

Over the space of the next half hour he identified several species he'd never seen in the wild before, some only from books. Hopping about the dunes were little grass wrens and tussac birds, at times coming within a few feet of where he sat. At the water's edge, a group of white-rumped sandpipers skittered back and forth on the glistening sand. A trio of oystercatchers flew in a sweeping arc and then landed. One clam-forager came very near to his left boot: either oblivious to Buster's presence or entirely too trusting of humankind.

After expending his reel of film and adding copious observations to his notes, Buster continued just to sit and watch them, transfixed with pleasure.

'C'mon David Attenborough,' Frank called from down the beach. 'It's scran time - Nobbay and me are starving!'

As they trudged back up to the settlement, Jenny fell-in between Buster and Frank, wanting to know what life onboard was like and what the three men all did. Bearing in mind the apparent gaps in the child's understanding of the contemporary world, the two men performed a kind of comedy double act. Keeping their answers more humorous than technical seemed to pay off, sending the child into frequent bouts of giggling.

As they approached the bunkhouse, Pam, who had been chatting with Nobbay, called to her sister, 'C'mon, small person, we have to go.'

The younger girl looked up at Buster and grinned, 'You'll come and find us tomorrow, won't you?'

'I suppose we will,' he grinned back, going along with whatever was going through the child's imagination.

Jenny performed another of her giggling pirouettes then skipped off to join her sister.

~.~

5

They arrived at the bunkhouse hungry. Nobbay drew the short straw to cook, and broke out the ration packs, selecting for the evening meal his personal favourite: steak & kidney pudding and mushy peas.

On the walk back, when asked about fuel for the stove, Pam had told Nobbay they kept the barn stocked with peat logs, and they could help themselves. Frank went out to fill a binbag with them but returned empty-handed.

'You havin' a laugh, Nobbay? There's bugger-all peat in that barn – in fact, it's completely empty.'

'We can always burn Nobbay's socks.' Buster said absently, busy loading a new reel of film into his camera.

'Maybe they've run out,' The PO Stoker muttered distractedly, struggling with a ration-pack can-opener and a tin of peas. 'Pam did say they were all going out to the peat field in the morning with a tractor and trailer. So, it'll have to be camp-- ah! *Youch!*' He examined his finger for blood, then picked up the dropped device.

'Oh, give it here,' Frank said.

~.~

After dinner, they took chairs from the hut and sat outside drinking beer as the sun lowered and shadows crept slowly down the western hillside. The breeze had dropped to a whisper, occasionally stirring the shrubs and bringing the scent of fresh-grown foliage to men more accustomed to the astringent aromas of the wild Atlantic.

'What's the plan for tomorrow?' Nobbay said, to no one in particular.

'Well, we're here to see wildlife,' Buster said. 'So, I guess that's the plan, I think we should go up that hill and see what's on the clifftop. What do you think, Frank?'

'Oh great, more bird watching.' Nobbay groaned.

Frank stirred from his reverie and looked across at him.

'Why did you sign up for this trip Nobbay?' he asked reasonably. 'It's obviously not your kind of thing.'

'Just to get off that grey bucket for twenty-four hours. I'd rather be here than on watch in that stinking engine room.'

The PO Stoker sounded gloomy, depressed. The persistent tic in his right cheek was a sign that all was not well in Nobbay's head. Buster speculated he would need to submit to some sort of counselling before long.

'There should be some sea lions over on the west side,' he suggested, keen to lift his messmate's mood.

'You'll like the sea lions, Nobbay,' Frank said, gently teasing, 'they're mean and cantankerous, just like you.'

Perceiving from his vacant stare that Nobbay was in no mood for the Welshman's ribbing, Buster changed the subject.

'I've been thinking about calling the ship,' he said. 'Report in about these people being here - they think this island is uninhabited.'

'Radio's for emergencies,' Frank said, pedantically. 'And this ain't no emergency.' Then he grinned and added, 'Quite the opposite, in fact; a cosy bunkhouse, a comfy bed, what more could a man ask?'

Buster was about to pursue his point, then paused. It was hard to disagree with Frank's argument to let sleeping dogs lie.

Later that night, burrowed in his warm sleeping bag on a bed free from ship's motions and sounds, Buster sank into a beautiful haze of wellbeing. Visiting a wildlife sanctuary in the Southern Ocean had been an ambition since before joining the navy. He relished the thought of a refreshing night's sleep before setting out on the journey of his dreams. But, behind these soporific thoughts lay the slumbering suspicion that all was not as it seemed in this island.

~.~

Buster woke to a vague feeling he'd been in conversation with a penguin. Frank's bed was empty, his sleeping bag unzipped and thrown open. Nobbay was still fast asleep, snoring gently from inside his quilted cocoon.

Shivering in the chill light of dawn, Buster padded across the room to fill the kettle and light the butane stove. The sunlight struggling through the dirt-caked windows did little to warm the room. Stepping briskly to the chair where his clothes were, he quickly buttoned his work-shirt over his thermal vest, then pulled on thick woollen socks, arctic combat trousers and boots.

The noisy rattle of Buster whisking dried milk in a tin mug caused Nobbay to stir. His weasel face emerged from the neck of the sleeping bag.

'What's the time?' he groaned

'Time to rise and shine, mate,' Buster said breezily, 'Sun's up and the day's a-wasting.'

Picking up his camera, he walked over and pulled open the hut door. The big man was fully dressed, sitting on a tussac watching the sunrise.

'What's up, Frank, shit the bed?'

Without looking around, the Welshman raised an extended middle finger, which Buster captured on film, beautifully silhouetted against a clear morning sky.

'Watch I don't shove that camera where the sun don't shine,' growled Frank.

Buster grinned. 'Tea's wet, mate, come and get it while it's hot.'

The big man stood, stretched, and walked back to the hut.

'I went up to the house to say hello and bum some fresh milk, but nobody answered the door.'

'They've probably made an early start,' Buster suggested. 'Farmers, y'know?'

'I never heard no tractor, and I sleep light. Besides, where do they keep it? It wasn't in the barn yesterday evening.'

Buster shrugged. 'Phew! Dunno, mate. Maybe it's somewhere else. Still, the island's only a couple of miles long so we'll probably bump into them at some stage.'

Nobbay had gone back to sleep. Buster strode over and shook him gently by the shoulder.

'C'mon Rip van Winkle, shake a leg. Tea's wet!'

Jerking awake, the PO Stoker swung out his legs and then sat there, still up to his neck in sleeping-bag, staring as if bewildered by his surroundings. He moved only to free an arm to take the mug of tea Frank had made for him.

Meanwhile, Buster set to making breakfast: tinned bacon with scrambled eggs, baked beans and oatmeal biscuits.

~.~

6

After breakfast, the men packed a few supplies from their Bergens into smaller rucksacks and set off to explore to the west and south of the island. A fresh westerly breeze had sprung up, but the sky was still clear; bright morning sunlight glinted off the sea behind them and warmed their shoulders.

They made their way up a slope lushly carpeted with lush green shrubs festooned with red berries. Curious as always, Buster stooped and rolled some into his palm. Gingerly, he tasted one: it was sweet and sharp; slightly bitter but not unpleasant.

'I wouldn't do that,' Frank said. 'The sheep have probably peed on em.'

Buster spat out what remained of the fruit, then spat some more, winning scornful chuckles from his shipmates.

They came to dip in the hillside in which lay a small pond. The rise beyond gave way to a prospect of the ocean to the north. The ducks and geese on the water seemed unperturbed by their approach, some paddling eagerly towards the visitors.

'Fresh meat,' Frank said. 'We should have brought rifles.'

'There wouldn't be much left of an upland goose after a 762 round's blown it apart,' Buster said.

'A bit more than in those rat-pack breakfasts,' Nobbay countered.

Frank said, 'What do you expect from a ration-pack, full bloody English?'

They made their way around the pond and up the sloping rocky shoreline. Occasionally on these lower slopes, they came across strange circular mounds covered in tiny white flowers like delicate lace, some rising to several feet. Close-up to them, Buster detected a faint aroma, indistinct but vaguely familiar. Vanilla, he decided. He made a note to find out more about this unusual flora from the sisters.

'Funny looking ant hills,' Nobbay said. He dealt one a hefty kick. 'Yow!' he cried, hopping away in pain.

'What a plonker!' Frank said, shaking his head.

Before long, the men reached a precipitous clifftop, not exceptionally high but sheer and rocky. The southern aspect afforded a view down to the opposite shore, which sloped away almost to sea level. They paused here while Frank unfolded a map from his thigh pocket.

'That's East Jowett Bay down there,' he announced. 'That's where they said the sheep are.'

Buster raised his binoculars. 'I see no sheeps.'

Frank asked, 'Hey, what did the shepherd say to his dog?'

'Dunno,' responded Nobbay. 'What did the shepherd say to his dog?'

'Let's get the flock out of here.'

Buster groaned.

'Ha-ha,' drawled Nobbay sarcastically.

They continued south near the cliff-edge, a moderate climb toward a blind summit. And now the men became increasingly conscious of avian crowding, a rising tide of shrieks and calls, at times, drowning out the wind and the crash of waves breaking below. Birds in their hundreds soared above the nearing horizon, wings flashing brightly in the sunlight. Then came the acrid stench of fish-laden guano. The source of this sensory assault was a small, rocky inlet, where the shipmates halted with jaws agape.

'Flamin' hell!' Frank said.

Nobbay was too stunned to speak.

Buster gazed on the spectacle with shining eyes. *This* was what he had come to see.

The cliff inside the bay stepped down to the swirling seas in a series of broad terraces. The whole edifice was crammed with seabirds, hundreds of thousands of seabirds, of staggering variety. They clung precariously to narrow ledges on sheer faces, waddled around on the level sections, floated on and flew above the churning waters, and filled the skies above the cliffs. They soared and dived and squawked and squabbled. The rich aroma burned sinuses and stung eyes – the rocks everywhere gleamed white with their droppings. And the noise was a clamouring onslaught on their ears.

Frank shouted out that it was like Alfred Hitchcock's The Birds. Nobody replied.

Presently, Buster was busily clicking away, expertly adjusting his telephoto lens. He shot terns in mid-flight, boobies feeding their young, guillemots squabbling on precarious ledges. There were cape pigeons, giant petrels, and snowy sheathbills, and many other species, all with young to feed, all nesting in the rifts and fissures of the cliff face. Here thrived a community of such magnitude and variety to make any naturalist's heart race like a jackhammer.

Recovering from his astonishment, Nobbay wrinkled his nose and grumbled, 'Jesus, Buster! Is this what yo've been going on about?'

But the Fenman merely threw him a shiny grin and carried on with his photography.

'It stinks worse than a Thai brothel,' Nobbay persisted, 'And I can't hear meself think.'

'Two good reasons for staying I'd say,' Frank laughed. 'But lets you and me move back a bit and give Bill Oddy here some space.'

~.~

Immersed in a single-minded drive to capture everything of this extraordinary pageant of nature's wonders, Buster lost all track of time. He was startled, therefore, when the Welshman walked up behind him.

'Hey! *Tempus fugit*, mate.'

Buster checked his watch. Christ! Had he been here an hour already? Reluctantly he stowed his camera. If he'd been alone, he reflected, he would gladly have risked sensory palsy to spend another hour making notes of this fabulous place. But the team had to stay together; that was the rule, it didn't need saying. Still, he had got some incredible shots.

Nobbay re-joined them, and they walked on.

'How did you get to be a twitcher?' Frank asked when they were far enough from the din to speak normally.

'Caught the bug from my Dad.'

Buster recalled childhood days, wading out in the misty-morning reed-beds to watch a pair of nesting marsh harriers or follow the booming song of a bittern.

'From when I was a nipper, he used to take me out on the fens. He taught me all the birds' names, including the Latin ones, how to recognise their calls, the whole shebang. It got so I was nearly as obsessed as he was.' He glanced at Frank and chuckled at the Welshman's expression. 'It's catching, so I wouldn't get too close.'

'God, I 'ope not.'

'It was all we ever talked about.' Buster continued, 'Sad, I know. Then one birthday he gave me a field guide and glasses, and I think it was that that got me started off my own bat.'

'A bit like me, really. My Dad played professional rugby, and as they say, the apple never falls far from the tree.'

Buster grinned, 'You don't see too many apple trees out on the green and crinkly.'

'So true, mate,' the Welshman said sadly.

'You know, Frank, when we're miles out at sea, and everyone off-watch is bored shitless, you know where I am?'

'I know where you go, Buddy. I've spotted you out on the Signal Deck. Never realised you were up there twitching though.'

'Yup, that's me. I spend my downtime with the boobies and the albatross and the stormy petrels.'

Frank laughed. 'Good for you, mate.'

Nobbay said, 'Oi think I'd rather be bored shitless.'

'Not difficult in your case,' Frank said, punching him lightly on the shoulder. 'With such a limited attention span.'

'Yo get stuffed!' Nobbay told him.

The three companions walked on under a crisp, clear sky, the southern sun doing little to warm ears and noses chafed by the chill breeze. They followed the line of the cliff's edge with the steel-blue ocean stretching away before them, her long swell thundering on the rocks below.

They stopped again at what appeared to be the island's highest point and took stock of their position. Out to the east, the red roof of the farmhouse stood out against the skyline. The house itself and outbuildings remained obscured by their surrounding hills. Beyond and to the left stretched the penguin colony and the beach they had visited yesterday.

The entire island to the west was now on glorious display—a rugged, rolling landscape of greens and browns with cutaways of exposed granite that sparkled in the raw sunshine. From this spectacular overlook, the cliff immediately ahead sloped steeply down to a vast field of tussac grass. The tussocks here were unusually tall, their topknot fronds waving in the wind, like a crowd of gorgons silently awaiting the judgement of Poseidon.

Beyond the tussocks lay the beach, where the shapes of several large animals could be seen. The remaining coast climbed steeply once more and gradually veered away southwards as if to protect the island from the full force of the ocean's storms. And at intervals along this coast lay sheets of flickering white which bristled with activity. These were the permanent nesting colonies of the island's many bird populations. Even at this distance, their chittering and squawking carried faintly on the wind. It was a wild and beautiful place that filled Buster with an extraordinary sense of freedom and optimism. The Navy seemed a million miles away.

They passed a narrow inlet in the cliffs, and reaching the farther side, they stopped to have lunch while observing yet another of nature's spectacles. The bottommost twenty feet or so of cliff opposite was sheer and unbroken. Above this, a series of jagged ledges led up another sixty feet to the top. In the boiling water below floated hundreds of penguins, their yellow-crested heads bobbing above the water: surfers looking to seaward for the Big One. When it came, the little birds were hurled with shocking violence against the cliff face. It was hard to imagine anything surviving such an impact. But incredibly, when the colossal wave receded, half a dozen penguins remained, furiously hopping up the ledges to escape the next deluge. The remainder were washed back into the water unharmed, and calmly awaited another attempt at landing.

'Amazing the little beggars don't get smashed to bits,' Nobbay observed.

'Now you know why they're called rockhoppers.' Buster said.

The men sat down on the smooth, sun-warmed granite of the cliff top and opened their lunchboxes to the unfolding drama. Many of the rockhoppers had now made it almost to the clifftop. A single orderly file had formed and proceeded to the final apex before turning right along the edge. Buster pointed out a weaving linear depression in the rock that passed close to where they were sitting. He wondered abstractly how many generations of webbed feet it had taken to wear that track into the durable granite.

In a moment of childish mischief, Nobbay swung his legs out across the path. 'I wonder if they'll go round me or hop over.'

'You'll probably get shat on,' Buster warned him.

The PO Stoker looked doubtful for a moment, but then shrugged. 'I'll risk it.'

The first penguin to come along the path stopped when it got to Nobbay's legs, and the queue began to bunch up behind. But only for a moment. Up the bird hopped, first onto one knee, then the other, then off the other side. The rest followed, and progress resumed: they were as unstoppable as a column of soldier ants. Sentient vermilion beads settled briefly on each of the men they passed, calmly accepting the novelty of strange animals along their route. Buster snapped off a couple of pictures for Nobbay to send home.

'Not bored now, Nobbay, eh?' Frank teased, settling his large thighs across a nearby rock.

For some reason, Nobbay seemed unable to reply.

Frank took out his map and checked their location.

'This place is marked as 'Circle Point', Buster. Thought you might like to name it in your journal.'

'Good idea, thanks.'

As Buster turned to watch the last of the departing penguins, he noticed something odd: the birds seemed to be deviating from their time-worn trail. Walking over to investigate, he discovered that a rockfall had wiped out an entire section of the original route.

And suddenly that weird feeling was on him again, lifting the hairs on the back of his neck. He felt once more that crushing wave of sadness, and this time, an ethereal whisper seemed to ride in on the wind. So profound was its effect that he felt light-headed and distant from his body. And like before, a second image seemed to shake out of the very air, a sepia version of reality.

Then, as quickly as it began, the moment was past. Buster wondered again whether he was coming down with something. Then he noticed the Welshman, standing and staring with the strangest expression.

'There!' Buster cried. 'You felt it, didn't you?'

'I felt something' Frank conceded in a voice of restrained awe.

Nobbay merely looked puzzled.

Buster stammered, 'Kind of ... weird? And a noise that might have been the wind--'

'No, not the wind, more like somebody whispering,' said Frank.

'Yes! Like a... like someone whispering... What else did you get, Frank?'

'Hard to describe really. Like I felt something move, but not like... Oh, I dunno. It's gone now anyway.'

Nobbay seemed unaffected by what Buster, and now Frank, had experienced. A fresh batch of transiting penguins was now absorbing the PO Stoker's attention, and he began muttering inanities like, 'Tickets please,' and 'Mind the gap.'

Frank and Buster simply stared at one another, trying to find words for something that had none.

'Hey, there you are!'

All three men looked up. Their surprise visitor forestalled any further discussion.

'Hi, Pam,' Frank called, 'Your sister with you?'

'Yeah, just coming.'

She reached down to scratch the head of a penguin that had stopped by her feet, then looked up and noticed Nobbay's legs obstructing their trail.

'You know they'll poo on you, don't you?'

'Nah,' Nobbay said. 'Why would they do that?' Then, addressing the bird who had just paused on his knee, he asked: 'Yo wouldn't crap on yer Uncle Nobbay, would yo?'

Pam grinned down at him, 'Oops! Looks like he already has.'

As the penguin vacated his knee, Nobbay saw the saucer-sized dollop of brown sludge it had deposited. He bent to look closer and immediately jerked back as the smell hit his nostrils.

'Aww, that's disgusting!' he cried, jumping to his feet and scattering the remaining penguins.

Holding the soiled trouser leg away from his knee, the PO Stoker looked around desperately for something to wipe off the guano. His shipmates were of little help: Buster had fallen onto his backside laughing, while Frank was reduced to bending over a rock and wheezing feebly. Pam stood like someone keen to retain their dignity in the face of absurdity. When Jenny skipped up and saw what was happening, she stopped and stared at the men.

'Keep back, Jenny,' advised her sister. 'They've all gone a bit mad.'

~.~

7

Buster eventually recovered sufficiently to find Nobbay a roll of paper towels in his rucksack.

Straightening and wiping laughter tears from his eyes, Frank asked the children, 'So, where did you two spring from?'

Jenny sidled up to her sister. 'This is our special place, this is where--'

'Huh! We're just down there at the peat stack,' Pam interrupted, pointing inland.

Buster looked, but could see nothing, and assumed the tractor must be hidden by the dip.

'We're helping Mam and Dad load the trailer,' explained Jenny, spinning about gleefully. 'We heard your voices, and we came to see if you--'

'Shut up, Jenny! It's not time.'

Seeing the young girl's stung expression, Buster fished a chocolate bar out of his ration pack and offered it to her.

Jenny looked at it longingly but didn't reach to take it.

'I can't,' she said sadly but did not elaborate.

Puzzled, he offered it to the elder girl, but she merely shook her head. Perhaps they were diabetic, Buster thought. But he didn't pursue the matter. It was none of his business.

'You live in an amazing place,' he told them. 'If I had kids, I'd bring them here like a shot.'

'Ooooh yes!' Jenny said excitedly, 'bring your children here, it would be so-oo much fun.'

'My kids wouldn't like it much,' Frank said, laughing. 'They think nature's boring.'

'We don't get many visitors,' explained Pam, mussing her sister's hair. 'Especially not other children. Jenny's just got me, and I'm getting a bit old to play her games.'

'And you're always doing your homework, or helping Dad,' complained Jenny.

Pam grinned ruefully, 'It has to be done, and pretty soon you'll have homework too.'

'Well, I'll promise you both something for what it's worth,' Buster said, feeling a little overcome. 'If I ever have a kid, I'll bring he or she here – what an amazing holiday. You two will be grown up by then, but I hope you'll remember me.'

'A she,' Jenny whispered, a dreamy look in her eyes.

'Pardon?' Pam said.

'He said he or she, he'll have a little girl. I just know it.'

'Wow!' Buster said, grinning hugely. 'That's a long shot. I'm not even married yet.'

Pam studied her sister for a moment, then turned back to address the visitors. 'Have you seen the sea lions yet?'

'Scary Sam and his wives!' cried Jenny.

'No, where are they?' Nobbay said, screwing up his nose as he rubbed at the stain on his combat trousers.

Jenny grinned when she saw what Nobbay's was doing.

'Ha-ha, penguin poo,' she said gleefully. 'Rub as long as you like, you'll never get rid of the stink till you wash 'em!'

Pam said, 'The big bull and his harem are down at Marmont Point.'

Buster nodded and saw a chance to glean some local knowledge. 'We saw some weird plants down by that little lake,' he told her. 'We wondered what they were, big solid mounds with small white flowers?'

'I nearly broke me foot on one,' complained Nobbay.

'Serves you right, shouldn't have kicked it,' Buster said. 'Any ideas, Pam?'

'That will be the balsam bogs at Otter Pond,' Pam said, grinning at Nobbay. 'It's what our island is named after. Mam hates 'em – she can't get the gum out of our clothes. The sea lions are down there through the tall tussac bogs. You'll see the cormorants on the way—'

'Cormorants?' said Buster.

'Don't worry, you can't miss them. Just follow the smell.' She crinkled up her nose to emphasise the point.

'Watch out for Scary Sam,' Jenny said, eyes wide and earnest. 'He gets *really* furious.'

'Yeah, good point,' Pam added, 'Don't let him corner you on the rocks, you can get quite close but keep your escape route in mind in case he charges.'

She took her sister's hand.

'Thanks for the advice,' said Frank. 'Are you two heading back down now?'

'Yeah, our Dad will be getting ready to leave,' Pam said. 'We drive up this way to go home, it's easier driving up here when the trailer's full, saves getting the wheels stuck down in the valley. C'mon, Jenny, we need to go.'

'Just a minute Pam,' Buster said. He walked with them a few yards down the hill where some of the red berries grew.

'Can you tell me what this stuff is?'

'Yeah, that's diddle-dee, we make jam with the berries.'

'Jam, really?' Buster said, stooping to roll off a few fruits into his hand.

'Yeah, really. Our jam's famous,' Pam said proudly. 'Waterton's Diddle Dee Jam. It's on the shelves at the shop in Stanley.'

A strange look came into her eyes when Buster popped a few berries into his mouth. He stopped chewing. 'What? They can be eaten raw, can't they?'

'Yes, they can,' she confirmed and looked away as if keen to be off.

But Buster had one more query. He looked behind to make sure the others were out of earshot, then asked her, 'Pam, do you get earthquakes here, or like, weird stuff happening, like, I dunno, air tremors or something like that?'

The girl looked at him for a moment, then grinned, 'We don't, but my Dad does when he's had too much whisky.'

Buster chortled. 'I know that feeling all too well.'

'Got to go now,' Pam said, her grin fading. 'You'll find us soon,' she added mysteriously.

'Yes,' enjoined Jenny, 'Find us soon, please!'

Buster watched the girls hurrying down the slope, the little one holding her sister's hand and occasionally glancing back at him.

Once again, he closed his mind to the thing that simply had no explanation.

~.~

8

When buster re-joined his mates, Frank was wearing a frown.

'Something very odd about those girls,' the Welshman said, looking down to where the sisters had disappeared. 'Don't get me wrong, they're nice enough kids, but somethin' just seems a bit off with 'em, you know?'.

'Yeah,' agreed Nobbay, 'must be living out here in the back of beyond with no mates. It can't do a kid's head no good.'

Buster thought the root of youngsters' odd behaviour went far deeper but made no comment.

After a moment's thoughtful silence, Frank gave a sigh and became business-like. He looked at his watch then consulted the map. 'Right, it's one o'clock now, pickup at sixteen thirty—Marmont Bay's only about half a mile. I reckon we can get there and back to the pickup point in about two hours. What d'ya reckon, leader?'

'It's a plan.' Buster agreed.

'Yeah, okay,' agreed Nobbay. 'Let's get down to the beach so I can wash off this muck.'

As they started out, Buster pointed out the rockfall he had discovered.

'Best not get too close to the edge,' he cautioned.

As the men stepped warily past the missing section of cliff, they noticed that the collapse had only been partial. The disappeared portion had merely slipped down, leaving a ledge a few feet below the clifftop.

'Whenever this happened, it wasn't recent,' Buster observed, pointing out the moss and grass that covered the wall exposed by the slip.

Frank stepped closer to the edge and peered down. 'There was definitely a fall though,' he noted. 'There's a flipping great pile of rocks down there.'

He stepped back and studied the rest of the clifftop surface then frowned.

'Do you suppose they'll be alright, bringing a tractor and trailer up here?' he said, kicking at an inch-wide crack in the sloping granite. 'Only it don't look too safe to me, heavy load like that.'

'The kids didn't seem too bothered about it when they walked this way,' Nobbay said. 'Sounds like they've done it loads a times before.'

Their Special Place?

What had the youngster been about to say, Buster wondered. He was sure Nobbay was right, but he also shared Frank's concern. Still, he reasoned to himself, the father would know whether it was safe or not and would doubtless make his own judgement before driving over it.

They walked on.

Pam had been right, the king cormorant colony did indeed smell bad, many times worse than anything they'd come across so far. Nevertheless, it was mesmerizing to see the spectacle of what Buster estimated was around five thousand breeding pairs. Each nest, built of grass and guano, contained one or more chicks. When Nobbay ventured too close to one of the nests, a vicious bill lunged at his legs. He quickly withdrew, but not before Buster had managed to capture the incident on film.

'Ho-ho, that'll be a good one to show the lads,' Frank said.

As they cleared the colony, even Buster welcomed the respite of leaving the noise and the stink behind.

Eventually, the ground levelled out, and the three men angled inland, entering the field of tall tussac 'bogs' they'd seen from the hill. Walking among them became quickly disorientating for Buster and Nobbay. It was a bewildering maze, and the two shorter men relied on Frank's superior height to navigate them through.

However, the tussac grass came with a dividend for Buster. Most of the fibrous root-clumps provided a home to some creature. Gentoo penguins made their burrows deep under the tussocks. A great many traversed the sandy trails winding between the columns, casting the men curious glances as they shuffled by.

Sooty shearwaters nested in the tussac roots; Smaller birds of all kinds skittered everywhere. As well as the ubiquitous tussac bird, there were many kinds of finches that Buster would have liked to spend some time identifying and studying. But they were short on time and keen to see the sea lions before returning to the pick-up point.

It was in this extraordinary place, among those strange and diversely populated columns, that Buster reiterated his promise to little Jenny.

'I meant what I said, you know, Frank? I'm coming back here one day, maybe when I've got kids; give my son the same inspiration Dad gave me.'

'Stop it, will you!' the Welshman said. 'You'll have me in tears in a minute.' He guffawed loudly before adding, 'Anyway, it's certain now, you're getting a daughter whether you like it or not – the Oracle said so.'

'No, I'm serious, this place is bloody amazing.'

'Yeah well, I've lost count of the number of times I've said I'll come back to some amazing place after I leave the mob. Even talked about it in the pub back home, but I doubt I'll ever do it.'

Buster too had made such vows, now all forgotten, but he knew this was different.

Occasionally they came across the dried-out carcase of a large animal, and Buster guessed these were the remains of seals. Some were so big that they could only be elephant seals. He wondered aloud if these plants, growing on dry sand without much organic foodstuff, relied on these carcasses for their sustenance, along with bird droppings and kelp.

'The dead feeding the living,' Frank whimsied. 'Very poetic.'

Nobbay imagined a sea lion a dog-sized animal such as he had once seen at Dudley Zoo (that mammal was, of course, a seal). So, when the engineer stepped out onto the rocky beach, the significance of the word 'lion' became suddenly and terrifyingly clear. In fact, as far as size was concerned, the term 'lion' did not quite cut it. Nobbay might have mistaken the beast for a nine-foot-high stack of washed-up kelp, had 'Scary Sam' not let out such a ferocious roar on seeing Nobbay emerge onto *his* beach.

On his dash back into the bogs, the engineer collided heavily with the Welshman coming the other way. With an explosive *'oomph'*, the smaller man sprawled backwards into a fibrous mound of tussac. Nobbay's terror was further compounded when a large albatross protested loudly from between his legs and began clacking at his boots.

'Don't panic yer daft sod,' the Welshman said, laughing as he dragged his shipmate clear of the tangle of grass and the slashing beak.

And thus ended another comical farce.

They chose an appropriate observation point on the rocks a little further along the beach and settled down to watch the animals. From here they had a clear view past the tussac field all the way up the cliff slope they'd walked down.

Buster turned his attention to the shingle beach, where the magnificent bull shuffled restlessly on his flippers. Covered in thick, dark brown fur with a great mane of shaggy chestnut hair, he quivered with muscle. Suddenly, he let out a roar to the sky, exposing long and impressive teeth to remind the visitors of their place on his beach.

Nobbay said, 'How am I going to get down to the water with that bloody thing there? These strides chuck up like a witchdoctor's juju bag.'

'Nothing new there then,' Frank quipped.

Buster looked at Nobbay and saw the resentment there. He turned to the Welshman, 'Frank, let's just cut the man some slack, eh?'

For a moment, Frank's face wore an injured look. But then he smiled ruefully.

'Fair enough,' he said.

'Just go further down, Nobbay,' Buster advised. 'As long as you stay off his bit of the beach, I'm sure you'll be fine.'

'Glad *you're* sure,' Nobbay grunted and set off to clean his trousers.

The bull's harem of seven females languished on the nearby rocks, and several young pups flapped around them. Offshore two more bulls looked on but kept their distance.

'You suppose those two are looking for a bit of the action?' Frank said.

Buster said he doubted the two smaller males were would-be interlopers. They were probably just juvenile males of the colony keeping a respectful distance from the domineering Alpha.

Nobbay returned with most of the mess removed from his trousers, only a pinkish wet patch remained.

Further down the beach, where Nobbay had carried out his ablutions, a family of kelp geese waddled ashore. The men laughed at the goslings tripping over their feet and each other in their efforts to keep up. Buster pointed out a large bird of prey soaring high above them and suggested it could be a turkey vulture.

'What, like in the shit-kicker movie?' Nobbay said. Then began a lusty rendition of the Eldorado song; a noise which would have been terrible even without the Black Country dialect.

Old turkey buzzard,
Old turkey buzzard,
watchin' and awaitin'
waitin' and a…

'If you don't put a sock in it, Nobbay,' gritted Frank, 'I swear I'll feed you to that sea lion.'

'You've got no soul,' Nobbay quipped, but mercifully sang no more. He seemed in better spirits now the faeces had gone from his trousers.

With their attention fixed on the activity in the sealion colony, the men started at a sudden rustling in the tussac bogs behind them. They turned around and watched apprehensively for what new terror would emerge. Suddenly, two steamer ducks scampered out. With an exchange of grins at their needless panic, they watched the two flightless birds waddle rapidly down to the beach and take to the water. The pair set out quickly to seaward, propelling themselves with thrashing feet and stubby beating wings.

They felt it before they heard it, a sudden vibration in the rock they were sitting on. When the sound came, a second later, it was a dull boom, followed by a prolonged rumble, not loud, and muffled by distance.

'What the hell was that?' Frank muttered.

'Earthquake, maybe?' Nobbay suggested, his voice an octave higher than usual.

'Look!' Buster said, pointing up to their right, 'Over there.'

A column of grey dust rose from the clifftop they had recently vacated, Circle Point. Buster locked fearful stares with his companions.

'Shit!' breathed Frank, scrambling to his feet, 'C'mon, let's get up there.'

~.~

9

To avoid the maze of the tussac field, the men decided to find a more direct route along the shore. Frank led the way, Buster, close on his heels, with Nobbay struggling valiantly to keep up. Scary Sam made a half-hearted charge but then hunkered down to watch the sailors run by as he got it that their objective lay elsewhere.

Clearing the edge of the tussac, Frank spotted a suitable embankment and shimmied up it, sending sand and shingle careering down behind him and forcing the followers to find their separate ways up. Succeeding to the lower section of the cliff, they continued upward with adrenalin-fuelled urgency. The dust cloud had now dissipated on the wind. Still, there remained the certainty that something terrible had happened, and the probability that people needed help. Buster dreaded what they might find up there; he pushed himself beyond what he'd thought possible, his mind on the fate of two young children and their parents. Visions of a tractor and trailer—

Damn! What if they've gone over?

He slowed to a halt - leaving the navy prop-forward to run ahead - and stepped to the cliff-edge, looking down along the line of crashing surf. The tide was down, exposing a narrow shingle shore at the base of the cliff. A jumble of large rocks lay at the bottom, below Circle Point, but he could not tell whether these were from the previous collapse or new fall. Nevertheless, from this viewpoint, a fallen tractor and trailer would be clearly visible, and there was no evidence of that.

The rest of the narrow beach was empty except for a few circling seabirds and some penguins in the water.

Nobbay caught up and joined him, doubled over and wheezing.

'Nothing down there,' Buster confirmed. 'C'mon, let's get up top.' He turned and sprinted on, leaving Nobbay staring hopelessly after him for a moment before following at a more sustainable pace.

~.~

Frank stood at the top of Circle Point looking down into a V-shaped crevasse where a further wedge of granite had fallen away into the sea.

'Got a torch in yer bag?' he asked as Buster ran up to join him. 'I think there's something down there.'

'Well it's not wide enough to swallow a tractor,' Buster observed, scrabbling in the bottom of his rucksack.'

He pulled out his flashlight and pointed it down into the opening. It was still murky with swirling rock-dust, but there was one prominent piece of evidence.

'Looks like there was a void,' he said, traversing the flashlight down the inner face. Strings of vegetation clung to the dark, glistening stone; stems and leaves pale and ghostly due to the starvation of light. 'Else that stuff wouldn't be growing there.'

'Yeah, I noticed that—'

Nobbay pulled up, panting heavily. 'What … what we got, then?'

'We were just saying this must have been some sort of cave,' Buster explained. 'Before it got opened by the rockfall. Doesn't look like anyone's come to harm though. Must have happened after the tractor passed.'

'Or maybe not,' Frank said. 'Hand me that torch, Buster.'

Frank shone the torch into the narrowing part of the fissure and trained it slowly downwards, then stopped.

'There! See that? What does that look like to you?'

'An opening,' said Nobbay. 'A tunnel, maybe?'

'Or just a ledge,' Buster said.

'No, you're not looking.' Frank flicked the torch sideways and back again. 'There, that bit poking out. *What's that*?'

'*Bloody hell!*' breathed Buster. 'Is that a boot?'

'Exactly,' confirmed Frank. 'And a small boot at that, and a trouser bottom. That's someone's leg, that is. A kid's leg.'

Buster cupped his hands to his mouth:

'HELLOO, CAN YOU HEAR ME DOWN THERE?'

'Anyone bring a rope?' Nobbay asked doubtfully.

'We didn't come to climb a bloody mountain, did we?' Frank snapped, growing angry and red-faced.

Nobbay held his tongue.

'HELLOO, IF YOU CAN HEAR ME, MOVE YOUR RIGHT FOOT'

'No, nothing,' Buster murmured.

'Right,' Frank said, slipping off his rucksack. 'I'm going down there.'

'Hang on, Frank,' Buster said. 'That's a bit risky without a rope. Why don't we just call for help?'

With a derisive snort, Frank pulled the portable radio out of his rucksack and handed it to Buster.

'You do that, mate. But you'll be lucky if the ship's in range, and the Lynx won't even be airborne yet.'

Buster switched on the portable and then stared up into Frank's desperate face.

'Try it if you want,' the Welshman told him. 'You might get lucky. But there's a kid in trouble down there, and I'm not willing to wait.' He glared defiantly at his team leader, 'No buts, Buster, I mean it.'

Buster shrugged. 'Okay, but just give me a minute to try. If they don't answer, you can go.'

Buster lifted the handset and pressed Transmit:

    'Mike Romeo, this is Foxtrot. Over.'

    …

Frank sat and dangled his legs over the edge and shone the torch down at the small boot and trouser leg.

...

'Mike Romeo, Mike Romeo, this is Foxtrot, d'you read? Over.

...
...

Buster gave a resigned sigh and switch off the radio.

'Okay, Frank. How do you want to play this?'

Frank removed his hat and scratched his head, frowning. The failed attempt to contact 'Mother' had given him pause to think.

'Well, I reckon I can get down there alright, there's plenty of hand- and footholds, but no way can I risk the climb back up with the kid on my shoulder.' He looked gravely up at his shipmates. 'Guys. We're going to need a rope.'

'Okay,' Buster said, 'Let's work through our options. We think there's a child down that—'

'We *know* there's a kid down there,' Frank corrected.

'Right. And where do we think the child's parents are right now?

Frank said, 'Hopefully, they're out looking for her.'

Nobbay said, 'Or maybe they haven't missed her yet - if she went off alone.'

'In which case, they might be at home,' Buster said. 'And think of this: we've never seen the two girls apart, so we can't exclude the possibility that they're *both* down there.'

Once again, Frank stared down into the crevasse.

'So, one of us needs to go down to the farm,' concluded Nobbay.

Buster nodded. 'Yup. So here's the plan. Frank, climb down with the First Aid kit and see what you can do for whoever's down there. Nobbay, you stay up here and look after him, and keep a good lookout for that tractor or anyone walking around. Also, give the ship a call every ten minutes – she shouldn't be too far away now. I'm going to run down to the farm and take it from there.'

'And bring back a rope,' added Frank.

'And bring the *tractor* up to help us,' said Nobbay.

'Good idea,' Buster said. 'Good luck, Frank, take it steady, yeah?'

With that, Buster set off, jogging down the hill through ankle-deep diddle-dee, sweeping up a handful of the berries to sustain him. He quickened his pace and struck inland to take a more direct route, his boots tossing up clouds of leaves and berries in his wake. He was glad of the action. Running this hard took his mind off worrying and pointless speculation about what had happened at Circle Point.

The huddle of buildings came briefly into sight at the summit of the balsam bogs and was hidden once more on the drop-down to Otter Pond. Ignoring a gaggle of upland geese, he startled into the air, he powered up the final hillock and paused at the ridge overlooking the farmhouse.

There was no movement around the farm - no sign of tractor or trailer either. Studying the little farmhouse, it occurred to Buster that, had he not seen its occupants with his own eyes, he would have sworn this was a place of dereliction and abandonment. It certainly had that look about it now.

Reaching the house, he knocked politely on the door.

Nothing. No noise except the squeal of seabirds and distant waves pounding the shore.

He knocked a little more insistently.

Nothing stirred.

A faint creak, then a wooden clunk sounded from nearby – it seemed to come from down where the barn stood.

Ah, that's where they are.

Buster stepped back and looked down at the tall structure. One of its two big doors was missing, the other hung drunkenly by one hinge and swung gently in the breeze. Odd that he hadn't noticed that before. The cavernous interior looked empty.

With growing apprehension, Buster stepped back to the door and battered it with his fist

'Hello, anybody home?' he shouted. 'Hellooo!'

Almost frantic now, he strode quickly to the barn. It was indeed empty, no rope, no tractor.

No people.

He ran back to the house and battered on the door again.

He tried the door handle.

Locked.

'Right, sod it!' he said aloud. Taking two paces back, he charged the door with his shoulder.

The door did not merely burst open; it collapsed onto the floor with Buster sprawled on top of it. Climbing to his feet, he peered into the dusty gloom, finding it hard to comprehend what his eyes were telling him. It was like a scene from another age. Most shocking of all; the whole place was thickly strewn with cobwebs. Nobody had set foot in this house for years, maybe decades.

~.~

10

Lying on his belly, Nobbay stared anxiously down into the crevasse. The Welshman remained sitting motionless on the ledge thirty feet below. Nobbay could see him quite clearly, and the big man seemed in no difficulties.

'What's happening down there?' he called for the third time. 'Is the kid alive?'

Nobbay's voice reverberated down into the dark depths. And *still* the big man failed to respond.

'Frank! Talk to me, mate.'

It had taken Frank almost an hour to shuffle down to the ledge. Nobbay thought he had heard a sharp intake of breath. Since then, the Welshman had just sat there, staring silently into the cave in the narrow end of the fissure. Occasionally, he would shine the flashlight into the cavity for a few seconds, then switch it off again.

Nobbay started when a heap of coiled ropes slapped onto the granite beside him.

'How's he doing,' Buster asked quietly, stepping to the edge and peering down. 'Is the child alive?'

'Dunno, he won't talk to me.'

'What do you m— Hey, Frank! You okay down there?'

There was a long pause, then,

'Not really, mate. You get a rope?' Frank's voice came up the fissure hauntingly distracted.

'Yeah, hang on a minute, I'll rig something up.'

'Okay, mate, take your time. There's no rush.'

The Welshman's words and the bleak tone of their delivery filled Buster with foreboding.

Buster had found two manila ropes in a storeroom at the back of the derelict house. These he now knotted together to give a total length of about fifty feet. Finding a rock pinnacle a few yards back from the cliff edge, he looped the rope twice around it and secured it with a bowline.

'Stand clear below,' he called down to Frank. 'Coming down.'

The rope clattered down between the rocks and hung a few feet below the ledge where the Welshman was sitting.

'Got it, that's fine,' Frank called, but made no move. He just sat there holding the rope.

'Up you come then, Frank. We're all secured up here.'

…

'Frank?'

'I don't like to ask this, fellas, but do you think one of you could manage climbing down here? I don't want to be the only one to see this.'

Buster looked across the divide at Nobbay. 'What do you think, ever done any climbing?'

Nobbay shook his head sadly and blew out his cheeks. 'I can climb a ladder, but that's about it. Wouldn't trust meself to go down a rope. Sorry, Buster.'

Buster found the descent remarkably easy - the unevenness of the crevasse walls provided adequate purchase and footholds. As he came within reach, the big man hooked him by the belt and heaved his backside onto the ledge beside him.

A cold, dank smell of decay and rotting vegetation permeated the air. The shelf was covered with a thick layer of sodden moss which quickly soaked through Buster's trousers. He could see nothing except the Welshman's solemn features, eyes glinting in the sparse light.

'Welcome to hell,' Frank whispered. 'Brace yourself for a shock, Bach. And I'd keep hold of that rope if I were you.'

Despite the warning, Buster almost lost it when the flashlight came on, and there, shining back at him were a pair of small human skulls.

'Awww! Jesus Christ!'

Buster averted his eyes and for a few seconds, swallowed repeatedly. When the vomit reflex subsided, he looked up at Frank.

'I did warn you,' the Welshman said. 'But you need to see it all.'

Despite his revulsion, Buster knew Frank was right. He and Frank's eye-witness testimony would be vital, and they must take in every detail of the grisly tableau. The circumstances that had brought about this tragedy was for later and for others to conclude.

He took the flashlight from Frank unresisting hand and began a visual examination of the cadavers.

Remnants of dark woollen clothing hung in shreds over the skeletal torsos of two small humans. Where ribcages were exposed, he observed a patina of pale moss on the bones. Water dripping from the cave roof had washed the skulls white, which was what had first shocked him. All that remained on the glistening carapaces were a few strands of sodden dark hair. He trained the torch down between the pair.

'Oh, Jesus!' he whispered. 'Look at that.'

The flashlight beam had come to rest on the merged bones of two small hands.

'I know,' Frank said. 'They died holding hands.'

He glanced at Frank, and in the deflected light, he saw the Welshman had been crying. Buster suddenly shivered and felt himself welling up. He understood now why the Welshman had lingered here in this dreadful place. And why he had wanted someone to share this with him.

'Listen,' Frank said quietly. 'What can you hear?'

Buster listened.

'I can hear water dripping.'

'No, not that. Shhh, listen.'

Buster listened and let his senses wander, feeling the soft sea breeze on his face. And now, on this gentle, caressing air came whispering voices like those he had heard this morning on the clifftop. And he picked out words, childlike murmurs, soft and fluting. They stood his neck-hairs on end and sent icy shivers down his spine.

'They're talking to us,' Buster murmured.

'I didn't understand what they were on about,' Frank said. 'All that business about findin' em. Now I do.'

Deeply moved, the two men kept vigil another five minutes, listening to the fluting voices.

Heaving a big sigh, Buster called up the crevasse, 'Nobbay, pull up the rope, will you, and send down my rucksack?'

'Okay,' Nobbay said. 'Then are you coming up?'

'Oh, Yes. It'll be just the two of us. And don't ask, we'll tell you later.'

'What's in the rucksack that you want?' asked the Welshman.

'My camera.'

'Buster, mate… you can't…'

'Just one picture. In case this is a crime scene.'

'Oh, never thought of that.'

Before leaving the children in peace, the two friends listened a little longer to the ethereal whispers carried on the breeze.

Thaaank Yoo… Thaaank Yooo

~.~

11

The helicopter came in low and fast and executed a showy landing two hundred yards from the house. Dressed once more in immersion-suits and life jackets, the three friends threw in their kit and climbed aboard, donning helmets and strapping in. Once all was secured, Buster plugged in his helmet and spoke to the aircrew.

'We're ready in the back Boss.'

Ogilvy stuck his head out to check behind then and slid his window shut.

'Clear to lift.'

As the helicopter lifted and tilted forward, Buster watched the farm with its red roof receding below, and once again felt that shifting moment as the colour drained out of the contradictory scene below.

As the Lynx banked sharply to port, Buster gasped. He nudged the Welshman, who tapped Nobbay so that all three rear passengers now stared out of the down-facing window in astonishment.

For there was Pam, with her little sister, Jenny. Behind them stood the two adults whom the men had seen yesterday. All four were smiling up and waving. Then the Lynx turned away, and they were gone from sight. But the ghostly image of that enigmatic family of Balsam Island would linger forever in the shipmate's memories.

'How was it, PO?' Ogilvy asked on the intercom.

'Great Exped Boss,' Buster said, trying to keep his voice steady. 'Highly recommended.'

They'd agreed not to mention their gruesome discovery to the aircrew. Tomorrow, Buster would ask for a meeting with the First Lieutenant so the authorities in Port Stanley could be informed of the bodies.

And the rest of what happened on that island? Well, that would remain a shared secret between the three shipmates.

~.~

12

April 2012

I knew now, of course, thirty years on, where Vimy Ridge was – it was in that spine of memory that remained of my grandad's generation. Remembrance Sunday: best uniform with medals, poppies (worn with pride), the Royal Marine Band playing Elgar's 'Nimrod'.

Vimy Ridge was the site in Flanders of a battle fought sixty years before my visit here with Frank and Nobbay. The father of those tragic girls - glimpsed in that fleeting moment after we landed, and again as we left - could not have been more than forty years old. That is why I had unfinished business here; a story untold that had nagged me down the years. My recent searches on Google and Wikipedia had proved fruitless, the information was too remote in time and place, too obscure to attract interest. Perhaps here, where for me it all began, I would, at last, discover the truth.

After breakfast, Heather and I donned our hiking gear and packed rucksacks for a full day's walking. The other guests had teamed up together and hired a guide for the optional Official Island Tour. That 'big group' experience was not for us.

We started at the Visitor Centre behind the lodge. Signs were pointing to galleries marked: 'Wildlife', 'Geology' and 'History'. Predictably, Heather made straight for the Wildlife section.

'I'll join you in a minute,' I said, heading into the History Gallery.

I looked at rows of old photographs, taken by families who had lived and worked here as sheep farmers from the late nineteenth century.

I spotted a series of news articles about the last family to live here, from 1920 to 1936. It was there I spotted it:

THE TRAGIC STORY OF
THE WATERTON FAMILY

Suddenly I was swept by a sensation I hadn't known for thirty years; a deep, unrelenting sadness, and a faint, familiar whisper. It was different now, less intense. It was a memory only, not the thing itself. Still, I found it nostalgically moving, and with a queasy feeling in my stomach, I read on.

PORT STANLEY TIMES
Monday 13th January 1936

Last Thursday 9th January the Waterton family of Balsam Island failed to check in on the evening radio roll call. Following several unsuccessful attempts to make contact with the outpost, the governor, HE Sir Hubert Hinton, ordered the dispatch of the Coastguard Cutter with 5 (five) constables to investigate. The house, farm buildings and surrounding area, were found to be deserted and the tractor was missing. A subsequent search of the island discovered the tractor and trailer at the bottom of the 60-foot cliff at Circle Point. The bodies of Donald Waterton (38), a veteran of the Great War and receiver of the Military Medal, and his wife Alice (35) were recovered. Of their two daughters Pamela (14) and Jennifer (8) there was no trace, and they are presumed drowned. It is believed they had been driving home along the cliff top when part of the cliff gave way. The family leave no surviving relatives. The Funeral, and a Memorial Service for the children, will be held at the Cathedral, on Friday morning at 10am.

A faded photograph of the Waterton family accompanied the article. A handsome couple and their two girls dressed up for a family portrait. The girls looked younger here but were easily recognisable. I pictured little Jenny performing that mad pirouette whenever something pleased her. And Pam, a protective arm around her sister. That solemn expression for the camera was a studied pose that I knew was apt to dissolve into fits of giggles if something amused her.

Underneath the article was a much later one, from the Penguin News dated 20th December 1983.

HUMAN REMAINS DISCOVERED ON BALSAM ISLAND

A forty-three-year-old puzzle was resolved last week when the remains of two missing children were recovered from a clifftop cave on Balsam. It is understood from MoD sources that sailors visiting the island last week made the discovery when part of the cliff collapsed, exposing the skeletal bodies of the two girls. The Government Police Unit were immediately informed by radio, and a team was assembled to recover the bodies. Post-mortem examinations carried out on Jenifer and Pamela Waterton (aged 8 and 14 respectively at the time of death) concluded no foul play was involved. The coroner has recorded a verdict of 'Accidental Death, probably due to exposure and/or starvation.'

Local geologist, Dr Henry Arkwright, who has subsequently investigated the site, said the girls were probably trapped inside the cliff following the rockfall that caused the family's tragic accident in 1936.

> 'There is evidence that there was a sea cave at the base of that cliff,' Arkwright told our reporter. 'Those poor girls most likely climbed up inside to get out of the water, but there was no way out at the top. Then another rockfall blocked the bottom entrance.'
> The two girls will be reunited with their parents when they are interred next Saturday morning.

I took out the picture I had shot while sitting with Frank in that grisly subterranean tomb. I had forgotten entirely about that photograph by the time I got around to getting the film developed. I recalled my conversation with the girl at the chemists.

'I'm really sorry,' she had said with a grimace. 'But this one seems to have been badly overexposed.'

I'd looked at the print she handed me and froze, not sure at first what I was seeing. As realisation dawned, I barely heard the assistant's next words.

'We've done our best with it; quite an arty effect, don't you think? Like an old Dutch master - children's faces staring out of the night. A bit spooky, though.'

I had no answer, just shook my head, unable to take my eyes off the print.

Seeing my expression, the girl frowned, 'Mm. Maybe not what you intended, I suppose. Once again, I'm so sorry.'

~.~

13

Leaving the Visitor Centre, I set off with my daughter up the footpath towards Circle Point. A fresh breeze came down from the slopes ahead of us, bringing with it the sounds of the distant shoreline: waves crashing onto the granite cliffs, the calls of myriad birds, and perhaps something else: a faint musical chime, recalling the laughing and chattering voices of two young girls. I pictured them running carefree in their exclusive and eternal playground.

At Circle Point, I left Heather snapping away at penguins with the camera I'd bought her for the trip.

Steel safety-railings had been fixed into the granite around the crevasse. A rough stone obelisk had been erected nearby among the diddle dee shrubs, engraved simply:

PAM & JENNY

Nothing else: no dates, no explanation. I thought it was perfect
and wondered who'd put it there. I took a last wistful look at my old photograph. Instead of the unspeakable horror of that cave, the developed photo was strange and wonderful. I smiled one last time at the cherubic faces of two sisters smiling out of the darkness. Then I buried that print deep in the peaty soil at the base of their memorial stone. And I don't know if it was all in my head, but once more I caught echoes of those haunting whispers.

Thaaank Yoo... Thaaank Yooo

I summoned Heather to walk with me and led her down the slope through the diddle dee; the entire hillside burned scarlet with their multitudinous berries. Bending down, I rolled off some fruits into my palm.

'What are you *doing*, Dad? They might be... you know, poisonous or something.'

I gave her a wink. She rolled her eyes, then shook her head in despair as I popped a few into my mouth.

'Here,' I said, handing her some. 'Just try them.'

I laughed at her crinkled-up nose.

'They're really quite nice,' I assured her, savouring the sweet, pleasantly bitter fruit.

'The people who used to farm here made jam out of them.'

~.~

About the Author

A life-long hobby-writer of poems, journals, and whimsical essays, Michael Rothery only began writing full-length fiction after his retirement in 2012. In previous lives, he served twenty-five years in the Royal Navy before starting up a successful computer software company. Michael now divides his time between his home in Elgin and cruising the Atlantic and Caribbean islands in his sailboat. He established his imprint, Weatherdeck Books, in 2015.

For more details visit: www.weatherdeckbooks.co.uk

Other novels by Michael Rothery

(Available at Amazon)
The Rosie Winterbourne Series
To Run Before the Sea
The Travel Agent

The Conflicted Bride
(To be published in Spring 2021)

Weatherdeck Books